# THE ADVENTURES OF
# CAPTAIN WAFFELLO
## TOASTY'S REVENGE

### BY AIDEN DENNIS
### ILLUSTRATED BY ANGIE BUTLER

Copyright ©2018 Aiden Dennis All rights reserved
ISBN-13: 978-0-9984157-2-7
Library of Congress Control Number: 2018949279
eBI Press

Publisher's Cataloging-In-Publication Data
(Prepared by The Donohue Group, Inc.)

Names: Dennis, Aiden. | Butler, Angie, 1979- illustrator.
Title: The Adventures of Captain Waffello. Toasty's Revenge / by
    Aiden Dennis ; illustrated by Angie Butler.
Other Titles: Toasty's Revenge
Description: [Queen Creek, Arizona] : eBI Press, [2018] | Authored by
    an 11-year-old, diagnosed with ADHD at age 5, to help other children
    stay interested and maintain their focus. | Interest age level: 004-
    008. | Summary: "Captain Waffello is a hero like no other. He's
    distractible, super silly, and determined to save the world from ...
    burnt toast? With the help of his side kick, Sir Rup, Captain Waffello
    sets out on an epic adventure to foil Toasty the Terrible's evil plot.
    The biggest challenge he'll face? Staying focused!"--Provided by
    publisher.
Identifiers: ISBN 9780998415727 (paperback) | ISBN 9780998415734
    (hardback) | ISBN 9780998415741 (ebook)
Subjects: LCSH: Heroes--Juvenile fiction. | Pancakes, waffles, etc.--
    Juvenile fiction. | Toast (Bread)--Juvenile fiction. | Distraction
    (Psychology)--Juvenile fiction. | Good and evil--Juvenile fiction. |
    CYAC: Heroes--Fiction. | Pancakes, waffles, etc.--Fiction. | Toast
    (Bread)--Fiction. | Distraction (Psychology)--Fiction. | Good and evil--
    Fiction. | LCGFT: Action and adventure fiction.
Classification: LCC PZ7.1.D4681 Ad 2018 (print) | LCC PZ7.1.D4681
    (ebook) | DDC [E]--dc23

This book is dedicated my great
grandma, G.G.

She always loved caring for little
kids and I hope I can pass that
dream on!

-Aiden

# NOTE TO PARENTS, TEACHERS, AND ALL YOU AWESOME CARETAKERS OF LITTLE ONES

Aiden, who has ADHD, wrote this story with kids like himself in mind – wiggly and easily distracted. We know it's tricky to keep kids interested in a book long enough to get through it, so here are few tips:

1.  **Brain & Body Breaks:** If you notice your child getting wiggly or losing attention, offer a brain and body break! Encourage your child to stretch, or jump in place, or grab a healthy snack.

2.  **Action Fingers:** When Aiden was little, he used to pretend his fingers were a little action figure! He'd hold his two fingers upside down and use them as "legs" to run, jump, and battle imaginary bad guys. He includes Action Fingers throughout the story so your child can play, too.

3.  **Questions:** Reading together can be a fun and interactive activity! Before you turn a page, ask questions such as, "What do you think will happen next?" or "Why did he do that?"

4.  **I Spy:** Try to play a quick game of "I Spy". Pick something on the page and see if your child can guess what it is (or let them pick something and you try to guess).

We hope you enjoy reading this book as much as we enjoyed making it!

- Angie Butler (Aiden's Mom and Illustrator)

Wait. Do you EAT waffles?
Cuz that's just WEIRD!

Hi kid! Um, what's your name, eh?

Cool name, but it doesn't sound very "super hero-ish." I think we should call youuuu...

**ACTION KID!!!!!**

Action Kid, we're about to go on an adventure! If you start to feel wiggly, it's okay to take a break. Just find a book mark and we'll be here waiting.

When I need a break, I train to bring down villains.

## TOASTY THE TERRIBLE

Toasty the Terrible is Captain Waffello's long lost brother. He used to be good ... until he was burned in a toasting tragedy. Now he's out for revenge! If he has his way, every toaster will burn, burn, BURN!!!!

**POWERS**    Smoke Screen
The Smolder

# BAD GUYS V

## TOASTETTES

The Toastettes are Toasty's evil mini-pancake minions. They say random stuff and use bananas and spatulas as weapons. They're more loyal than smart.

**POWERS**
Bananarang
Spatula Smackdown
Soaring Spatula

So, about that adventure... basically, Toasty the Terrible and his Toastettes are trying to rig all the toasters on the whole planet.

They're so evil that they want everyone to burn their toast EVERY. SINGLE. TIME!

# GOOD GUYS

## CAPTAIN WAFFELLO

Our legendary superhero is silly, kind, smart, and SUPER distractible. His mission is to save the world and make you laugh and ... wait ... he just saw a puppy. Hold on just a sec ... he's petting the puppy now.

POWERS    Toaster Throwing ✳✳✳
          Terrible Puns ✳✳✳✳✳

## SIR RUP

Captain Waffello's handy side kick and number one fan ... Sir Rup! Sir Rup is organized and kinda derpy in a totally lovable way. His goal in life is to help Captain Waffello stay focused on saving the world!

POWERS    Organizing Stuff ✳✳✳
          Syrup Slinging ✳✳✳

And we're just over here trying to save the world from burnt toast like the heroes we are
...

But we need your help, Action Kid!

# FIND THESE OBJECTS

Oooo! Toasty's Evil Lair! I left my yo-yo there a long time ago. Can you find it, Action Kid?

Don't forget, Captain Waffello, we're trying to save the world here, eh!

# EVIL PLOT

1. FINISH MY TOASTER RIGGING MACHINE.

2. PUSH THE BIG RED BUTTON.

DO NOT PUSH!

3. RIG ALL THE TOASTERS IN THE WORLD TO BURN TOAST!

IMPORTANT: STOP WAFFELLO BEFORE HE GETS TO YE OLDE TOASTER FACTORY AND TRIES TO STOP ME!

MAZE OF DOOM

CALAMITY OBSTACLE COURSE

SECURITY CODE PUZZLE

1

BIG AL'S GROCERIES

2

YE OLDE TOASTER FACTORY

3

TOASTY

Aw, sweet! You found Toasty's Evil Plot. Good job!

Toasty has stationed his Toastettes at 3 different checkpoints, guarding Ye Olde Toaster Factory.

We must get through them to get to Toasty and stop him from pushing the Big Red Button!

Are you ready? We KNEAD to stop him. Let's go!

Action Kid! Use

# Action Fingers

to help Captain Waffello and Sir Rup get to Checkpoint 1.

16

STOP

BIG AL'S

1

GROCERIES

STOP

BIG AL'S

GROCERIES

STOP

PTHHHHHST

Forget the cereal. Focus, Waffello... FOCUS!

I've got it! I'll bamboozle him with a TERRIBLE PUN!

Captain Waffello's pun was so
bad that the Toastette fainted.

Good job, Captain Waffello.
We knew you could do it!

Now, let's keep moving.

23

# NICE!

You blew all the leaves off the trees and stunned the Toastette.

29

Action Kid! Use

**Action Fingers**

to help Captain Waffello and Sir Rup get to Checkpoint 3.

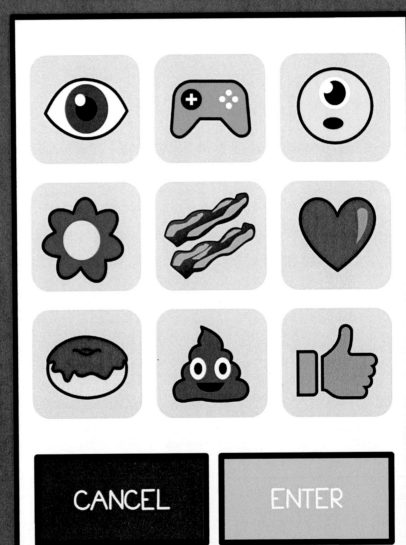

30

33

Well done Waffello, but you are too late! Let's see if you can handle the SMOLDER!
DO NOT PUSH!
TOASTY

Sir Rup, NOW!
While Captain Waffello is distracting Toasty, Sir Rup swaps the wires on Toasty's Big Red Button. I wonder what will happen NOW!
You can slow me down but you'll never stop me!
SLAM!
DO NOT PUSH!

37

You see, Action Kid, what Sir Rup did was cross the wires so that when Toasty pressed the Big Red Button, it ruined his plan and made the toasters work better than ever. Now they will always toast to perfection!

Thank you, Action Kid! You helped us save the world from burnt toast. We couldn't have done it without you!

Hey Sir Rup, can we go back to Big Al's and get that cereal now?

# SAY WHAAAAT? HOW DID AN 11 YR. OLD BOY WITH ADHD WRITE THIS BOOK?

Here's how it went down...

One morning Aiden was eating a waffle. After a few bites he looked down and said, "Hey mom, it looks like a face! It's a waffle AND a fellow. I shall call him Waffello." From that moment on, we've spent months working on getting this epic tale ready for you.

Aiden's writing process is different than some kids. He has a hard time staying focused when he works on any project. For all Aiden's writing - either for school or for this story - we first brainstorm ideas for 15-20 minutes at a time and make notes. Then once the arc of the story or the idea is ready, Aiden writes small pieces at a time.

For this book, once Aiden relayed his ideas to me, I'd illustrate them with no words. He'd look at the illustrations, ask for changes, and then write in the dialog a few pages at a time.

When he finished a section, we would share it with his younger cousins, Grace and Julian (ages 8 & 6), to see if they liked it or lost interest. These two incredible, goofy, neurodiverse kiddos know all about getting the wiggles and giggles, so we figured if they liked it, it might work for you, too. We also consulted with a clinical psychologist to get ideas and advice. Dr. Giselle Crow helped us with age-appropriate interactions, and with the notes at the beginning.

After several months, some frustration - you might think a book by a kid would have grammar and spelling mistakes, but every publisher makes their authors work with a good editor! - and lots of laughter and excitement, we are happy to share the result of his hard work. We hope his story is as inspiring to you as it was to us.

- Angie Butler (Aiden's Mom and Illustrator)

# ACKNOWLEDGEMENTS

We would like to offer a huge THANK YOU to the many people that helped make this book possible:

First, Dr. Giselle Crow, Clinical Psychologist, Long Beach, CA, for your consultation, ideas, and professional input which helped us shape this book into a fun experience for kids with ADHD/ADD or other similar challenges.

We'd also like to thank **Grace and Julian**, ages 8 and 6 respectively. They read sneak peeks of the book as it evolved and helped us make it better by giving us their honest opinions. We love you G&J! (BUTTNANAS!)

To **Ginny Heenan**, for being a mentor and a sounding board — we couldn't have done this without you! Thank you for your help, patience, and encouragement throughout this process.

And finally a HUGE thank you to all of our **friends and family** who listened to us go on and on about the book, contributed their thoughts and ideas and helped make this a fun and rewarding experience for us.

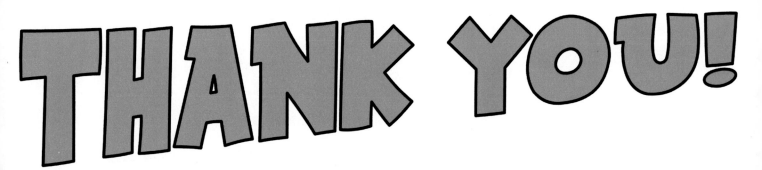

If you enjoyed this story and would like a free audiobook version to listen to while following along, use this QR code to sign up and download today! This bonus is available for a limited time.

## UPCOMING BOOKS FROM eBl Press:

Pre-order the next volume of The Adventures of Captain Waffello at a special pre-order price! Use the QR code to order today.

Use little-known secrets from math and science to train your brain to find 4-leaf clovers! Use this QR code to pre-order your copy of **How to Find 4-Leaf Clovers Using Secrets from Math and Science** at a special price today.

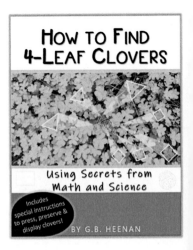

82496818R10024

Made in the USA
San Bernardino, CA
16 July 2018